Kaye

QUINTON QUEST
HUNTS THE YETI

Illustrated by Judy Brown

Catnip

CATNIP BOOKS
Published by Catnip Publishing Ltd
14 Greville Street
London EC1N 8SB

This edition first published 2008
1 3 5 7 9 10 8 6 4 2

Text copyright © Kaye Umansky, 1992
Illustrations copyright © Judy Brown, 1992

The moral rights of the author and illustrator have been asserted

A CIP catalogue record for this book is available from the British Library

ISBN 978-1-84647-057-8

Printed in Poland

www.catnippublishing.co.uk

CHAPTER ONE

*In which Sir Quinton introduces himself,
his cup, his butler, his wife and his newspaper*

Hello there! I am Sir Quinton Quest, the
world famous explorer. You've heard of me,
of course. Who hasn't?

Exploring has always been my passion. Even as a small baby, no play pen could hold me. Yes, I certainly displayed my roving spirit at an early age. I think I can truthfully say I crawled where no baby has ever crawled before.

See this? One of my proudest possessions. Explorer Of The Year Challenge Cup, presented by SOFE (Society Of Famous Explorers, of which I am a proud member). Not to be confused with Sofe the tea lady, ha ha. I've won this

delightful cup five years running. That's
a record. All the other explorers are jolly
green with envy, but as I always point out,
it's no more than I deserve. When it comes
to exploring, I'm your man.

This is Muggins,
my butler. I take him
with me on all my
little jaunts. He loves
exploring. Wouldn't
miss an expedition for
anything.

This is Lady Cynthia Quest, my good wife.

She prefers to stay at home.

But enough of them. You'll be wanting to hear about my famous Yeti quest. In some ways, it turned out to be one of my most interesting expeditions, although of course I never did see hide nor hair of a Yeti. Not that I ever expected to, of course.

It all began one morning when I picked up the *Daily Explorer*. I have always taken the *Explorer*. I write a lot of complaining letters to it.

Also, it's got a nice easy crossword.

Across

2. Sharp instrument used by explorers to cut a jungle path.

3. What explorers prefer not to do when up a mountain.

Down

1. What explorers like to do.

4. Used by explorers for drinking soup.

Besides, I enjoy reading Tip Of The Week. In fact, I've sent in several Tips Of The Week myself. Had several published, too. One of my better ones was "Save On Huskies. Take Your Butler". Many people have since thanked me for that. However, when I opened the *Explorer* on this particular morning, little did I know what awaited me . . .

CHAPTER TWO

In which Sir Quinton gets a horrible
shock and almost cancels his subscription

The Daily Explorer

SCOOP! THE YETI EXISTS!

Findley Ffoothold, that up and coming, popular young explorer, has recently returned from the Himalayas with astonishing new proof that the Yeti exists! Ffoothold claims that the photograph below is a GENUINE Yeti's footprint. A spokesperson from SOFE is quoted as saying "This could be enough to win young Ffoothold the coveted Explorer Of The Year Challenge Cup" blah blah . . .

Horror! The entire front page was devoted to that young upstart Findley Ffoothold – my explorer rival!

Bunkum! Balderdash! Tosh, tripe and piffle! That's what I thought about that! How dare the *Explorer* publish such rot! I almost decided then and there to cancel my subscription. (I didn't, but only because of Tip Of The Week.)

I examined the photograph carefully. "Genuine Yeti's footprint" indeed! That young whippersnapper Ffoothold wouldn't know a Yeti's footprint from a whale's armpit.

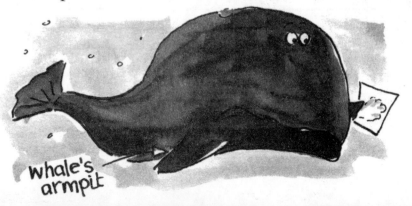

whale's armpit

The photograph was obviously a fake. I knew Ffoothold. A sight too big for his disgracefully overpriced climbing boots, if you ask me. The young pup's ambition knew no bounds. Why, once I even found him sitting in MY CHAIR at the Explorer's Club! Unbelievable!

I knew he had his eye on my Explorer Of The Year Challenge Cup and would stop at nothing to win it! Well, I wasn't going to let him.

Then and there, I decided to go to the Himalayas and see for myself. If the Yeti did indeed exist, I would come back with bigger, better photographs. Probably even an interview.

If I found nothing, I would expose Ffoothold for the rotter he is. Let's face it. He's not even a proper explorer. More a trumped-up mountaineer. To be a real explorer, you need the following:

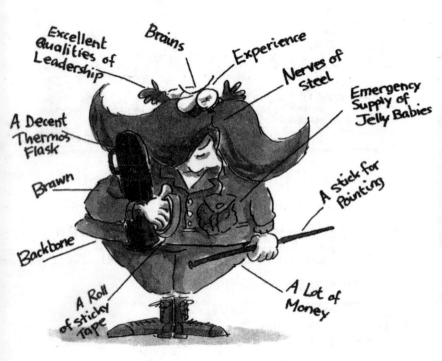

Excellent Qualities of Leadership

Brains

Experience

Nerves of Steel

Emergency Supply of Jelly Babies

A Decent Thermos Flask

Brawn

A stick for Pointing

Backbone

A Roll of sticky Tape

A Lot of Money

Naturally, I've got all of them. So who better than I to come up with the evidence? If, in fact, such evidence existed . . .

CHAPTER THREE

In which Sir Quinton makes a list

There was no time to be lost. The first thing
I did was make a list of essential items of
equipment.

List Of Essential Items

AA card (in case sleigh breaks down)
Alarm clock
Antifreeze
Aqualung (in case I have the misfortune to fall through ice)
Axe
Baked beans (NOT curried variety – tell Lady C)
Barometer
Batteries
Bed
Binoculars
Blankets (four, plus electric one)
Boots (fur-lined, make sure
    Muggins cleans them)
Boot polish
Bow-tie
Brandy (for medicinal purposes)
Brush and comb
Butterfly net
Camera (don't forget film)
Camping stove
Candles

Candelabra
Cardigans (NOT one with knitted chicken
Cereal (Bran balls, choc flavoured)
Chicken soup
China
Chocolate (drinking and bars of)
Chronometer
Coat (warm)
Cocoa
Cologne
Compass
Cooking utensils
Cutlery
Diary

Dinner jacket (get Muggins or Lady C to press)

Dressing gown

Duvet

Electric generator

Emergency supply jelly babies (don't forget)

Essential reading material: Deserts – Miles O'Sand
Explorer's Guide – Ivor Mapp
Hell On Ice – Torville & Dean
Mountains – Ben Nevis
Jungles – Tarzan

Extra bow-tie (just in case I lose other one)

Film (don't forget camera)

Flag

Folding table and chair

Fridge (small)

Gramophone (don't forget records – see V)

Grappling hook

Ground Sheet

Hammock

Hankies

Headache pills

Hot water bottle

Iron

Ironing board

Kettle

Knife

Maps

Matches

Mirror

Mittens

Monocle (spare)

Moustache net

Moustache wax

Mug

Needle and thread

Oil lamp

Pen

Pencil

Pencil sharpener

Photograph of Lady Cynthia (NOT the one of her squinting)

Pitons

Pyjamas

Roll of sticky tape

Rope

Sandwiches (pref. smoked salmon. NOT cheese and tomato)

Scarf (woolly)

Sextant

Shampoo

Shirts (clean. Muggins or Lady C to iron)

Sick pills

Skates (tell Muggins to polish)

Skis (ditto)

Sleeping bag
Sledge
Slippers
Snow shoes
Soap on rope
Socks (1 doz. prs)
Stamps
Sticks for rubbing together (in case matches get damp)
Stick for pointing at things
String (ball of)
Sunglasses (in case of snow blindness)
Swimming costume (in case plane comes down over sea)
Table-cloth
Talcum Powder
Tea bags
Telescope
Tents (one for me, one for supplies and, space permitting, one for
    Muggins)
Thermometer
Thermos flask (large)
Tins (tell Muggins to take plenty)
Toilet rolls (soft for me, hard for Muggins)
Toothbrush
Toothpaste
Torch
Towel
Tray (leave choice to Muggins)
Trouser Press
Umbrella
Vests (warm with sleeves. NOT itchy one)
Victor Sylvester gramophone records
Washing-up liquid (leave choice to Muggins)
Wine
Wine glass
Woolly hat
Woolly jumpers
Writing materials
Yeti horn (I suppose)

CHAPTER FOUR

*In which Sir Quinton plans the route,
Muggins packs and Lady Cynthia
makes a private telephone call*

I presented Muggins with my list.

He thought it a little long, but as I
explained to him, we explorers like to be
prepared. One never knows what one might
need.

I ordered Muggins to get on with the packing. I, of course, planned our route. Route planning is most important.

Lady Cynthia spent a great deal of time on the telephone booking our flight. She's always so helpful at these times. It really is jolly sporting of her. I consider myself most fortunate to have such an understanding wife.

Preparations took all day. I felt quite exhausted. I gave Muggins and Lady Cynthia their final instructions, then retired to bed, reflecting that I needed to be up bright and early the next morning.

But before I went to sleep, I wrote the title of my new journal.

I always keep diaries of my expeditions. Lady Cynthia will tell you they make fascinating reading.

The Yeti! What a strange image that word conjures up! Otherwise known as the Abominable Snowman, this elusive beast has haunted the dreams of us in the Explorer's Club for many years. Although those of us with a modicum of common sense firmly believe there is no such creature, we have all at some time or other fantasized about being the first to find one.

From time to time, reports come back of giant footprints in the snow. Young upstarts claiming to be explorers (Ffoothold, for example) claim to have fresh proof. The Explorer's Museum is awash with such so called "evidence".

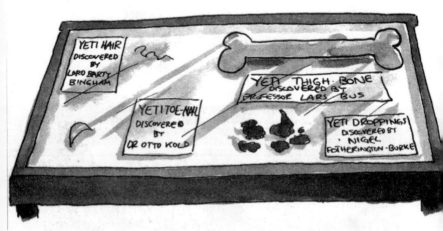

Poppycock! Fakes, the lot of 'em. Make no mistake about it. If the Yeti exists, there is only one person with the right combination of cunning and experience to track it down.

Me!

CHAPTER FIVE

*In which Sir Quinton breakfasts
upon kippers, toast, muffins, eggs and a large
pot of tea before departing for the Himalayas*

As instructed, the following morning,
Muggins woke me at the crack of dawn.

I thought he looked a little crumpled
and red around the eyes, and told him so. If
there's one thing I can't stand it's sloppiness.
He informed me he'd been up all night
packing.

Good, loyal chap – and keen as mustard. No excuse for standards dropping, however.

First, I took a long, hot bath – my last chance before entering on a life of hardship.

I then ate my breakfast and made helpful suggestions as Muggins and Lady Cynthia stowed the equipment into the car.

After an uneventful journey, we arrived at the airport. There was a bit of a fuss about the luggage, but I soon showed them who was boss.

Muggins and I posed for a final photograph before boarding the aeroplane ...

... and at long last, we were airborne. Lady Cynthia waved until we were out of sight. I hoped she would get the bus home all right. The poor woman misses me terribly when I go off on my little jaunts. Ah well. That's one of the penalties of being married to a world famous explorer ...

CHAPTER SIX

*In which Sir Quinton and Muggins arrive at the
Himalayas and find positively no sign of the Yeti*

At long last, we arrived at the foot of the
Himalayas. It was cold, bitterly cold, The
thermometer registered sub zero.

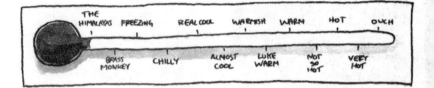

My monocle froze over in seconds, and
Muggins put a scarf on.

The plane took off, and we were quite, quite alone. All around was the wild, frozen waste, broken only by the odd pine tree.

Off we set. I led the way, of course. As we went, I took a great many photographs of the snow, just to prove that there were POSITIVELY NO FOOTPRINTS. Muggins followed behind with the supplies. What a stout fellow he is . . .

(NOTE: For the benefit of readers who are unfamiliar with the Yeti language, a translation has been provided)

Hi there! Sorry interrupt. Yeti here. In Yeti language, me called Squiggle Pine Tree Wiggly Line. But you can call me Bob.

See that? Me standin' 'round mindin' own business when big iron bird fly down and coupla weirdos get out bird's tummy. Little hairy fat bossy one and tall thin one who do all work. Weirdos got lotta stuff with 'em. What for, me wonder?

What weirdos want?

Why they here?

Me decide play detective and follow. All this snow 'round, nothin' else better to do.

CHAPTER SEVEN

*In which Sir Quinton and Muggins
make camp and try their hand at waltzing*

We walked all day. Soon, night fell and I
ordered Muggins to make camp. This took
some time, as there were the tents to erect, the
fire to light, the provisions to unpack and the
dinner to cook. I urged Muggins to make haste.
All this exploring gives one a raging appetite.

At last my tent was up. Whilst Muggins
busied himself with menial tasks, I dressed
for dinner. I always dress for dinner on
expeditions. It's good for morale.

After my meal, I instructed Muggins to wind the gramophone. I always like a little dance after dinner. I find it aids the digestion.

I felt much better after a bite to eat and a waltz or two. Muggins proved quite good at following my lead. I recall thinking that perhaps tomorrow night we might try the quickstep. But suddenly, the events of the day caught up with me and I was overwhelmed with exhaustion. I left Muggins to clear up and retired to my tent.

I regret to say that Muggins had failed me. Despite specific instructions, he had forgotten to place my pyjamas next to my hot water bottle! I made a mental note to have a word with him about that in the morning.

I was tired, darned tired. It was as much as I could do to undress myself. In fact, I called out to Muggins to come and give me a hand, but he didn't seem to hear.

Somehow, I managed it. But before I gave way to sleep, I forced myself to write up the first day's entry into my journal so that none of the fascinating details would be lost.

CHAPTER EIGHT

*In which Sir Quinton's thoughts turn
to home, Muggins writes a postcard
and the Yeti's thoughts turn to grub*

Day One
Got up at crack of dawn. Light breakfast of kippers, toast, eggs, muffins and a large pot of tea. Went to airport. Cynthia came to see me off. Touch of tummy trouble, probably all the excitement. Landed in Himalayas 15.30 hours. Everywhere snow, snow, quick, quick, snow! (small joke). Walked in snow all day. Set a fair pace. Muggins hard pressed to keep up. As I thought, no sign of Yeti. Pitched camp. Muggins cooked dinner. Waltzed. Decided to have an early night. As I lie here in my sleeping bag, my thoughts turn to home. I wonder what Lady Cynthia is doing right now. Knitting me another cardigan? At her flower arranging class, perhaps? Organising a jumble sale? Weeping over her solitary mug of bedtime Horlicks?

Whatever it is, I'm sure she'll be thinking of me . . .

With those fond words, I closed my journal. Outside, darkness had fallen and a blizzard was blowing up. I hoped Muggins had managed to erect his tent successfully. It was going to be a wild night. I could hear the roar of vast avalanches in the distance.

But it takes more than a little bit of noise to keep me awake. Unlike poor Muggins, who tells me he is a light sleeper.

Dear Mum,
Having an awful time. He's making me do all the work as usual and the tent's too small again. Please reserve that Careers book for me at the library. It's v. cold here, although I am wearing my scarf. Outside I can hear vast avalanches which

MRS MUGGINS
BETHNAL GREEN
LONDON
ENGLAND

Hello. It me again. Bob. Sorry interrupt, but that no avalanche. That me roarin' in triumph! Look what me found! Grub!

Yum yum. That what we Yeti's like best. Me get stuck in.

But wait! This too good to keep to self. Me greedy, but not THAT greedy.

Me go get relations.

CHAPTER NINE

*In which Bob goes to get his relations
and does a comic turn*

Me go to secret cave up mountain where we Yetis
live. Me give relations big surprise. Me say, "Hey!
What you think of outfit?"

Relations cluster round and admire. Me tell
'bout big iron bird. Relations spellbound at my
charismatic performance.

When me tell about weirdos, relations die
laughing. Me make real show of it. Relations think
me real comedian.

Last of all, me tell relations about grub.

That do it. Relations can wait no longer. Me lead way to weirdos camp. Me draw veil over next bit.

CHAPTER TEN

*In which disaster strikes
but Sir Quinton copes brilliantly*

I awoke the following morning, feeling
much refreshed after a quiet, uneventful
night. It was then that Muggins came
hurrying into my tent. He was wild eyed
and gesticulating. I guessed he had some
bad news.

I was right. Disaster had struck! Wolves
had got into our supply tent! All
that was left was a tin of baked
beans. There was nothing else
for it. I would have to tighten
my belt and ration myself to two
beans a day – one for breakfast, one for
supper. What Muggins would do for food I
couldn't imagine.

Of course, there was my secret
emergency supply of jelly babies,
but I decided to keep quiet about
those.

I didn't intend to let this set-back spoil
my plans. I had come to do some serious
exploring, and serious exploring was what I
was going to do. After my breakfast bean, I
decided what equipment I would take with
me.

It is most important to select wisely, as
one's very life hangs upon such things. After
much deep thought, I selected the jelly
babies, a map, a magnifying glass,
my camera, my stick for pointing,

a compass, my binoculars and a thermos of tea. And a roll of sticky-tape, of course. After some hesitation, I also took the Yeti horn.

The Yeti horn. Hmm. To my mind, a rather silly contraption which Lady Cynthia ordered as a birthday present from the Explorer's Catalogue. I must admit being rather surprised at her choice of gift, particularly as what I really wanted was a hot air balloon. Of course, I didn't say so. I didn't want to appear ungrateful. Unfortunately, Lady Cynthia does have a tendency to be taken in by advertising.

Explorers! When you next venture into the Himalayas, don't leave home without your Yeti Horn! It makes a sound which Yetis simply cannot resist. One blow, and if any Yetis are in the area, you'll know it all right!

The manufacturers claim that it makes the Yeti's love call. A likely tale! I mean, a non-existent creature can hardly have much of a love call! I didn't really want to bring it, but didn't want to hurt Lady Cynthia's feelings.

"Don't forget to try out the Yeti horn I bought you, dearest." Those were her last words to me. Then she turned and went back home alone to do some knitting or feed chicken soup to poor people or something. What a dull life the poor woman leads.

Ah well, enough of her. Back to me.

I instructed Muggins to stay behind and guard the one remaining precious tin of baked beans with his life.

Guard this tin with your life, Muggins.

I thought he looked rather glum. I offered to post his postcard for him, seeing I was going out, but he said he hadn't finished it. That'll teach me not to put myself out for the hired help in future. Feeling slightly annoyed, I left the camp.

CHAPTER ELEVEN

In which Sir Quinton has an unfortunate accident

It didn't take long before my mood lifted. This, of course, is what we intrepid explorers enjoy most. Out in the wild, alone. Facing peril fair and square. Using our wits and experience to battle with the elements. Laughing in the face of danger.

Remember what I told you an explorer needs? Brains, brawn, cool head and so on? Well, I certainly needed them now. I boldly struck out across the white wasteland. One false step, and it could be the end of me.

But I'm an old hand at this sort of thing. I know what sort of things to avoid, and what to watch out for. This is where experience comes in useful.

As I walked, I carefully examined the snow for the slightest signs. Hair, droppings, a footprint . . . anything really. But no. Nothing. Just as I thought. I took several more rolls of film as evidence.

So intent was I on looking for footprints,
I confess I failed to notice the precipice.
A small mistake but, as it turned out, a
disastrous one.

It could have been even worse, mind.
I was lucky. My foot caught in a small
branch or something, and I dropped
harmlessly onto a ledge below. When the
blood had drained from my head and
my stomach had rejoined my body, I
scrambled back up.

It had been a frightening ordeal. But I didn't allow it to unnerve me. As all good explorers should, I kept a cool head and inspected what was left of my equipment.

There wasn't a lot of it. My map and compass had been lost down the precipice. So had my camera, my magnifying glass and my binoculars. My thermos flask was leaking tea all over my socks. However, all was not lost. I still had my jelly babies, my stick and, thank heaven, my roll of sticky tape. Oh, and the Yeti horn. Mustn't forget that.

I had intended to head back for base
camp. But, having lost both map and
compass, I was unsure of the direction. Yes,
I was lost. But, being a true professional,
I naturally knew what to do. Somehow, I
must alert Muggins to my predicament.

I tried shouting, but to no avail.

I had no idea that the
Yeti horn would be so loud.

I personally doubt that it was me blowing it that caused the avalanche. I still maintain it was coincidence.

However, there was a rumbling and a crashing and an unpleasant shivering sensation . . .

Then all went white and I knew no more.

CHAPTER TWELVE

In which our hero is rescued and taken back to the Yeti cave

Can you believe this? Little fat weirdo frozen solid. What we goin' to do?

Oh well. First things first. It lunch time now. Time to knock off. Time to take loot back to cave and get stuck in. We Yetis take lunch time seriously. Important Yeti rule: never make decision on empty tummy. Eat first, make minds up later.

Weirdo grub delicious. Make nice change from pine needles. We all have HUGE lunch. Full tummy good thing for Yetis. It put us in good mood. It make us want to sing happy songs . . .

And dance . . .

And do cave paintings . . .

. . . and tell jokes. We Yetis happy types. We very fond of jokes

Yes, we Yetis love good laugh. Best of all, we like practical jokes. We remember time coupla months ago when *FIRST* weirdo come. We play lotta tricks on him. That good fun.

We drop snowballs on his head.

We make HUGE footprint in snow.

We mess him about something rotten. Ho, ho, what a laugh that was. But enough of trip down Memory Lane. Me suddenly remember little fat weirdo propped up outside. It time him goin' home before he catch worse cold. Me kinda fond of him. Him very smooth and slippery. Him slide nicely. We push him off down mountain. We aim him at base camp. We Yetis dead kind-hearted, really.

CHAPTER THIRTEEN

*In which Sir Quinton, against all odds,
manages to crawl back to base camp*

How I ever managed to get back to base
camp I will never know. I certainly have
no memory of it. I can only assume that,
against all odds, I somehow crawled. What
an incredible feat. What a tribute to my
stamina and grit.

It is just as well I arrived when I did. Back
at base, poor Muggins was beginning to
lose his grip. When I came round from my
faint, you should have heard the nonsense
he came out with. Some cock and bull story
about being trapped in his tent by a pack
of wild animals, can you believe? He even
claims one of them ate his postcard!

The poor chap was quite deranged. Came out with a terrible load of old drivel. Claimed I was FROZEN SOLID when I arrived back. Reckons he had to chip me out with a pick axe and thaw me in front of a fire. Me! His leader!

"Muggins," I told him kindly. "That cannot be. If I had been frozen solid, I wouldn't have been able to crawl, would I?" But the poor, deluded fellow couldn't see it. I took no notice of his wild babblings. It was obvious that he was suffering from temporary snow madness. Needless to say, he had missed my leadership. He was pathetically pleased to see me and greatly relieved when I took charge again.

Regretfully, I decided that we must leave immediately. Our supplies were sadly depleted, and a great many essential pieces of equipment were missing, including my stick for pointing. Now, that was something I couldn't do without, particularly in my weakened state.

Besides, it was blooming cold.

CHAPTER FOURTEEN

In which Sir Quinton and Muggins
struggle back to the plane stop
and resign themselves to a long wait

Keep going, Muggins! Mush!

The way back was long and hard, but somehow I managed to keep Muggins going. Finally we reached the plane stop. According to the timetable, there was a plane due. Of course, as we all know, that doesn't mean that one will actually come. Usually you wait and wait for weeks and weeks, then three land at once. We settled down for a long wait. I kept myself warm by writing in my journal.

Muggins read a book.

A CAREER IN LORRY DRIVING

CHAPTER FIFTEEN

In which Sir Quinton and Muggins are homeward bound

What a welcome sound! The roar of an approaching aeroplane. What's more, it wasn't full! Imagine our joy! Gleefully, we flagged it down.

We were even more delighted when we realised it was a proper one, with a charming hostess and an in-flight movie and sick bags and hot food and so forth. I

ordered lobster thermidor and champagne
for myself and a fish paste sandwich
and a small glass of weak lemon squash
for Muggins. I felt he deserved a little
something after his ordeal.

I was, of course, disappointed that our
expedition had to be cut short. I had
intended that we should be gone for
at least three weeks, and here we were
returning after only two days. However, I
soon cheered up when I thought of Lady
Cynthia, and how thrilled she would be at
my unexpected return.

She would have written to me by now, of course. A long, affectionate letter about her jam-making activities and pottery class. With any luck, I could be home before she posted it, thus giving her a lovely surprise and at the same time saving the cost of a postage stamp.

Do stop joggling me, Muggins.

To be quite frank, I was looking forward to a quiet time being waited on in the comfort and peace of my own home. As I have said before, these expeditions can be very tiring, even for an experienced professional like myself.

Above all, though, I felt that I had done what I set out to do. I had examined the Himalayas very thoroughly, and had found not a single scrap of evidence to support that young bounder Findley Ffoothold's wild claim.

At the first opportunity, I planned to stride into the Explorer's Club and laugh in Ffoothold's face.

I would present him with my photographs of plain, smooth, mint condition snow and ask him what he thought about that!! He wouldn't like it, but that was just too bad.

Yes, I'm pretty sure the Explorer Of The Year Challenge Cup will be mine again this year. What's more, nobody can say I don't deserve it. After all, I, Sir Quinton Quest, have proved beyond any shadow of doubt that

THE YETI DOES NOT EXIST.